Who BlowS the Wind

RAVEN KARLA WELCH REITHMEIER

AuthorHouse™
1663 Liberty Drive
Bloomington, IN 47403
www.authorhouse.com
Phone: 1 (800) 839-8640

Published by AuthorHouse 12/14/2018

ISBN: 978-1-5462-7289-2 (hc)
ISBN: 978-1-5462-7191-8 (sc)
ISBN: 978-1-5462-7190-1 (e)

Library of Congress Control Number: 2018914722

Print information available on the last page.

authorHOUSE®

"Much Honor to all of our Ancestors and Elders.

To my sons, Jared, Josh, and James Ryan, my Angels in disguise. To my many beautiful grandchildren and all of my "Mama Raven" kids, no matter if you're red, yellow, white, or black.

To my nieces, nephews, relatives and dearest of friends.

To our human race, to know we borrow the future from our children and are entrusted caretakers of Turtle Island, known now as America.

That 7 Generations from now, our Prayers are for All of our children, that they may know life giving and clean water and air, and be Blessed with the beauty of a Natural World that we are still able to enjoy for our present time. To remember we are to protect the Earth for future generations.

My Prayers are for life contuince for all to know Love, Faith, Hope, Charity and Unity for all tribes of Humanity and for the preservation of our Mother Earth.

Aho"

One day Little Brother was walking thru the woods like he did every day. This day he noticed a tree he had passed by many times before.

"Mr. Tree," said Little Brother, "I need your help so I can find out who blows the wind."

"Who told you that you could talk with trees, boy?"

"My heart told me," Little Brother answered.

"I know the wind. I feel its power as well as its gentleness, "said the tree, "but I am not the wind, boy. I only know what it is to be a tree."

"What is it to be a tree?" Little Brother asked.

"As a tree, I've learned to be still. I know the changes of the seasons, the colors of fall, the coldness of winter, the newness of springtime and the warmth of summer. Everything always changes. Through it all, I grow stronger, so I know to be still," said the tree.

Little Brother tried to be still like the tree. As the wind blew harder, storm clouds gathered and rain began to fall.

"The rain may know who blows the wind," said the tree. "Go, now, and ask the rain."

"Thank you, tree," said the boy. "See you later."

As Little Brother walked away, he felt the gentle rain trickle down his skin.

"Excuse me rain," said Little Brother. "I need your help so I can find out who blows the wind."

"Who told you that you could talk with rain, child?"

"My heart told me," Little Brother answered.

"I know the wind, but I am not the wind. I only know what it is to be rain," said the rain.

"What is it to be rain?" asked the boy.

"As the rain, I've learned that when I give of myself others will grow, and when storms happen, rainbows are sure to follow," said the rain. "Look, there it is beginning to form."

Little Brother tried to see the rainbow through the storm.

"The rainbow may know who blows the wind," said the rain. "Go, now, and ask the rainbow."

"Thank you, rain," said the boy. "See you later."

As Little Brother moved on, he could see the rainbow more clearly than before in the storm.

"You are so beautiful," said the boy. "I need your help so I can find out who blows the wind."

"Who told you that you could talk with rainbows, son?"

"My heart told me," Little Brother answered.

"I know the wind, but I am not the wind. I only know what it is to be a rainbow."

"What is it to be a rainbow?" Little Brother asked.

"As a rainbow, I've learned to pull all colors together. I know one is not more important than another. Without all the colors, the rainbow would not be beautiful.

It is my job to show how wonderful colors can be, side by side," said the rainbow.

Little Brother, wished he knew how to pull all colors together like the rainbow.

Soon sunset began to fall quietly over the sky.

"The wind must surely know who blows the wind," said the rainbow. "Go, now, and ask the wind."

"Thank you, rainbow," said the boy. "See you later."

The wind began to blow with both power and grace.

"Excuse me wind," said Little Brother. "I need your help so I can find out who blows the wind."

"Who told you that you could talk with wind, young man?"

"My heart told me," Little Brother answered.

"I am the wind, child. I can only tell you what it is to be wind."

"What is it to be wind?" asked the boy? "As the wind, I've learned when I blow with power and anger bad things happen. So I try to be calm, to create peace. I am free to be how I want and so are you, boy," said the wind.

Little Brother tried to be calm, to create peace like the wind. In that moment, he felt the gentle breeze blow lovingly through his hair.

"How am I going to find out who blows the wind?" asked Little Brother.

The wind paused a moment and answered softly. "Boy, you could speak my language and that of the tree, the rain and the rainbow because you've learned to trust and listen to the wisdom of your heart," spoke the wind. "Go, now, and ask your heart for the answers you need."

"Thank you, wind," said Little Brother. "See you later."

All at once the wind blew proudly, the tree shook with joy, the rain wept and the rainbow beamed.

"Excuse me, heart," said Little Brother, "I need your help so I can find out who blows the wind."

"Hello boy," whispered his heart. "The spirit of the wind blows the wind, child."

"Who is the spirit of the wind?" asked Little Brother.

"The spirit of the wind is the spirit in all living things. It is known by many names on earth, child, and it shows itself to us in many different ways," whispered his heart. "You learned today from the tree, the rain, the rainbow and the wind."

"I did not know before that I could listen to trees or rain or rainbows or the wind," said Little Brother.

"They are life's greatest teachers," whispered his heart. "You've seen that every living thing you meet knows something you don't. To learn, you need only to listen to that still quiet voice inside and you will understand with the truth in your heart.

"Thank you, heart," said Little Brother. "See you later."

Little Brother thought for a minute and understood he could learn many things from others but for the most important questions he needed to ask his heart.

Printed in the United States
By Bookmasters